Copyright © 1996 by Nord-Süd Verlag AG, Gossau Zürich, Switzerland
First published in Switzerland under the title *Tatü der kleine fremde Kater*
English translation copyright © 1996 by North-South Books Inc.

First published in the United States, Great Britain, Canada,
Australia, and New Zealand in 1996 by North-South Books,
an imprint of Nord-Süd Verlag AG, Gossau Zürich, Switzerland.

Distributed in the United States by North-South Books Inc., New York.

Library of Congress Cataloging-in-Publication Data.
Lachner, Dorothea.
[Tatü der kleine fremde Kater. English]
Look out, Cinder!/ Dorothea Lachner; illustrated by Eugen Sopko;
translated by Rosemary Lanning.
Summary: When Cinder, the little black cat, runs away from a huge red
"monster", she's lonely, far from hom, and wondring if her new neighbors
will ever be her friends.
[1. Cats—Fiction. 2. Frienship—Fiction]
1. Lanning, Rosemary. II. Sopko, Eugen, III. III. Title.
PZ7.L1353Lo 1996
[E]—dc20   95-36757
A CIP catalogue record for this book is available from The British Library.
ISBN 1-55858-520-6 (trade binding)
TB 10 9 8 7 6 5 4 3 2 1
ISBN 1-55858-521-4 (library binding)
LB 10 9 8 7 6 5 4 3 2 1
Printed in Belgium

Dorothea Lachner

Look Out, Cinder!

Illustrated by Eugen Sopko

Translated by Rosemary Lanning

North-South Books
New York / London

There was once a little black cat named Cinder who lived
all alone in a big city. Though she was small, she knew how
to look after herself, and at night, when the streets were
empty and quiet, she would prowl around looking for food.

The best place to look was the back door of the supermarket,
and tonight she was in luck. Someone had left the shutter
open, just a crack, but she could easily squeeze through.

Just then a huge red monster came howling and screaming
out of the darkness. For a moment Cinder was frozen with fear.
Only the tip of her tail quivered. Then she turned and ran, faster
and faster. Ahead of her loomed a black hole, like a cave.
She raced inside.

The cave door slammed shut behind her. There was another slam, then a rumble, and the cave began to rattle and shake. Cinder cowered in the darkness as the noise and movement went on for hours—*rumble, rumble, rattle, shake.*

Then all of a sudden it stopped.

A door opened.

At last she could escape!

But she didn't know where she was.
Everything smelled, sounded, and looked
strange. She wandered through the streets,
searching for a quiet corner where she could
rest and decide what to do. Suddenly she heard
a fierce growl. A big tortoiseshell cat glared
down at her from the top of a wall.
"Go away!" it hissed. "I'm Doremi,
and this is my territory."

Cinder fled into an alleyway. It smelled good, like the yard behind the butcher's shop. And there, on a piece of crumpled paper, was a scrap of meat. She was tiptoeing toward it when—*snatch!*—an orange paw shot out and whisked the meat away.

"That's mine," hissed an angry ginger cat. "I'm Marmaduke, and any food around here belongs to me."

Hungry and tired, Cinder crept under a dark staircase
and went to sleep. But not for long.

Another menacing voice woke her: "Get out of here!"
it growled. "I'm Silver Tiger, and that's where I sleep."

"And so do we," hissed Marmaduke and Doremi.
"We were here first. You don't belong here."

Sadly, Cinder wandered a safe distance away.

The next morning Cinder followed Silver Tiger, Marmaduke, and Doremi to a park. When they stopped and began to wash themselves, Cinder washed herself too. Now her fur looked clean and shiny black—except for a small grey patch that she tried to hide with her tail. When a small dog stopped and stared at her, the little cat tried to hold her tail steady—to look brave, like Silver Tiger—but it wouldn't stop trembling.

Then Cinder watched Marmaduke hunt.
He was the best mouser she'd ever seen.
She tried to copy him, stalking silently,
then pouncing, just as he did.
But the mice got away.
    That made the other cats smile.

At night, when darkness crept over the rooftops and the rest of the town went to sleep, the three big cats made music. They sat on the highest roof and crooned to the moon. Doremi had the best voice. Cinder tried to copy him. She climbed on a roof and meowed as loud as she could, but the other cats didn't seem to notice.

As the weeks passed, Silver Tiger, Marmaduke, and Doremi stopped chasing Cinder away, but they still didn't take much notice of her. If they spoke to her at all, it was just to say, "Get out of my way," or "Scram!" So Cinder slept alone, with only the moon for company.

Then one night the red monster came back, roaring, flashing, and howling.

Cinder screamed with fright. The tip of her tail trembled and she ran. She scrambled onto a crate, leaped from the crate to the top of a wall, and was just about to jump into the yard below when . . .

"Stop!" yelled Marmaduke.

"Don't jump!" called Doremi.

"Look out for the dog!" said Silver Tiger.

Now that Cinder was in danger, they realized how much they had grown to like her. They all ran over to the wall where Cinder stood trembling with fear.

"Come down," they said. "You can be our friend."

After that, the four cats spent all their time together, hunting, playing, and singing. When they all sang at once, they made a beautiful noise.

And whenever a fire engine, an ambulance, or a police car roared past, with its lights flashing and siren wailing, the others looked after Cinder so she didn't get frightened and run away. They didn't want to lose her. They would have missed her too much.